Retold by
Marcia Williams

WALKER
BOOKS

Contents

In which a tangled web is woven.

Orsino, Duke of Illyria, was lying on a couch, listening to his lute player's doleful ballads while dreaming of the countess Olivia. "If music be the food of love, play on, give me excess of it," he sighed. The countess, who lived close by, consumed the duke's thoughts both day and night. He was quite hopelessly in love with her. Unfortunately for Orsino, Olivia was in

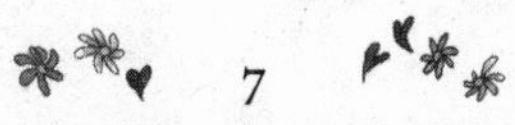

mourning for her dead brother and had sworn to allow no men into her house, or her thoughts, for seven years.

"Will you go hunt, my lord?" asked Orsino's servant Curio, hoping to distract his lovesick master and get away from the lute player's serenading.

"O, when mine eyes did see Olivia first, methought she purg'd the air of pestilence!" sighed Orsino.

Curio threw up his arms in despair – truly, if his master preferred the countess to hunting, he was beyond saving!

The previous night, there had been a terrible storm over Illyria, and although the duke knew nothing of it, a ship had been wrecked on the rocky coast below

his castle. One of the few survivors was a gentlewoman named Viola who had been aboard the vessel with her twin brother, Sebastian. Sebastian had vanished in the waves and Viola feared he was drowned. Poor Viola was now alone in the world, with no money. So the ship's captain advised her to dress as a man and seek work at the court of Illyria's ruler, Duke Orsino.

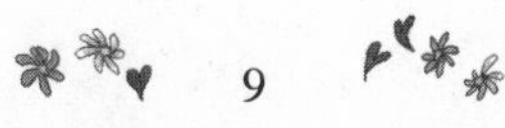

Dressed in doublet and hose, Viola made a convincing young man. She could sing mournful love ballads very beautifully, so Orsino was delighted to employ her as his page. Over the following days, he found his new page gentle and soothing to his lovesick heart, and he soon came to trust Viola above all his other servants. "I have unclasp'd to thee the book even of my secret soul," he sighed to Viola, after telling her of his love for the countess Olivia.

Orsino asked his new page to try and

woo Olivia for him, as the countess had refused to let him, or any of his other servants, into her house. Viola was most reluctant to take on the task for, since arriving at the castle, she had gradually fallen in love with Orsino herself.

"Say I do speak with her, my lord, what then?" asked Viola.

"O, then unfold the passion of my love," cried the duke.

"I'll do my best to woo your lady," Viola assured him. Yet what she really wished to do was to throw off her page's attire, put on a beautiful dress and capture Orsino's heart for herself!

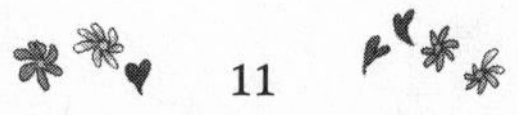

As Olivia would not allow men into her house, Viola was turned away on her first visit. But as she had promised Orsino she would deliver his message, she refused to move from the gate. Even when Olivia's rude steward, Malvolio, offered a dozen excuses why Olivia would not see her, Viola stood her ground. Finally Malvolio returned to Olivia, his feathers thoroughly ruffled.

"Madam, yond young fellow swears he will speak with you," he declared. "I told him you were sick ... I told him you were

asleep. What is to be said to him, lady?"

"What kind o' man is he?" asked Olivia.

"He is very well favoured and he speaks very shrewishly," grumbled Malvolio.

"Let him approach," said Olivia, who was growing bored of her own company.

As soon as the handsome young page entered Olivia's room, her heart lurched. She listened enraptured as Viola, on behalf of her master, began to praise her.

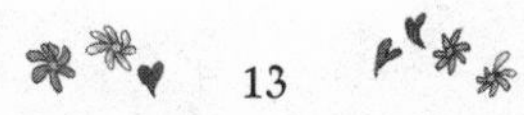

"Most radiant, exquisite, and unmatchable beauty," the page began.

Eventually, Olivia felt obliged to try and silence this outpouring since, as she explained to Viola, she did not love Orsino and never would.

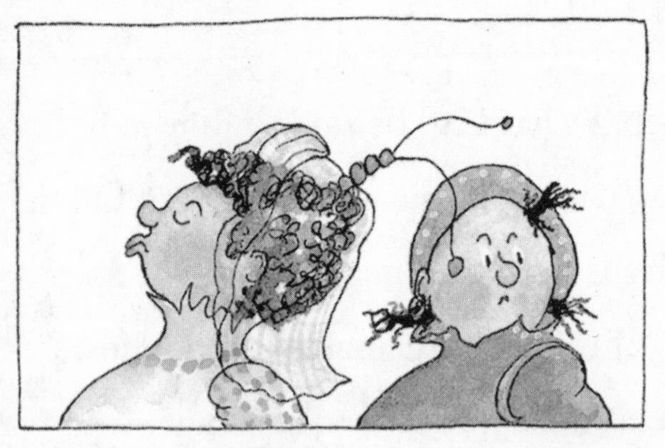

"I pray you, keep it in. I cannot love him. Let him send no more," cried Olivia. "Unless, perchance you come to me again..." For Orsino's page had flattered Olivia so delightfully that her heart had gone

from lurching to loving! "How now!" she whispered to herself. "Even so quickly may one catch the plague? Methinks I feel this youth's perfections with an invisible and subtle stealth to creep in at mine eyes."

Viola left the countess with a heavy heart. Olivia had rejected the very thought of loving Orsino, and her curt dismissal was likely to make her master weep. As Viola wandered slowly home, pondering how best to break this news to the duke,

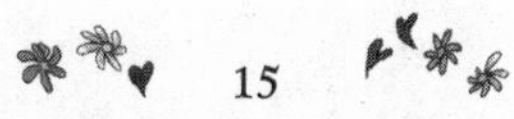

Malvolio came puffing up behind her.

"Were not you even now with the countess Olivia?" he gasped.

"Even now, sir," replied the page.

"She returns this ring to you, sir," said Malvolio.

Viola knew at once that the ring was not hers, but a love token from Olivia. She was mortified to think that Olivia had believed in her page's costume and, thinking her a

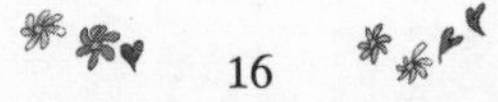

man, had fallen in love with her. She wished she could reveal her disguise, but then she would be without work or money.

Viola tried to refuse the ring, but peevish Malvolio just threw it at her feet and walked off.

"Poor lady, she were better love a dream," sighed Viola, as she stooped to pick up the beautiful ring. "Disguise I see thou art a wickedness."

As much as she would have liked to, Viola could think of no way of untangling this confusion without revealing her true identity.

In which Malvolio is tricked.

That night, the countess Olivia went to bed early, dreaming not of Orsino but his page. However, her maid, Maria, her jester, Feste, her uncle, Sir Toby Belch, and his friend, Sir Andrew Aguecheek, all stayed up late revelling and drinking. Sir Toby hoped that Sir Andrew might marry Olivia, for although he was much older than her, he was very rich and kept Sir Toby well supplied with wine.

As the night wore on, they reached that stage when voices begin to slur into song and every note seems perfectly pitched.

"*O mistress mine, where are you roaming? O! Stay and hear; your true love's coming*," sang the jester as he swayed back and forth.

"A mellifluous voice, as I am true knight," declared Sir Andrew.

"A contagious breath," declared Sir Toby, pouring more wine.

"My masters are you mad?" cried Malvolio, bursting into the room. "Have you no wit, manners nor honesty but to gabble like tinkers at this time of night?"

Sir Toby protested that a servant had no right to talk to him in such a way, but Malvolio would have none of it. He ended their revelry and packed them all off to bed.

The next day, the angry revellers decided to pay Malvolio back for spoiling their fun, and came up with the perfect plan.

As Malvolio walked about the garden, they dropped a letter in his path which Maria had written

in Olivia's handwriting. Just as the tricksters hoped, Malvolio picked up the letter from the ground. "By my life," he cried, "this is my lady's hand!"

As he started to read, his excitement grew, for it was a love letter! As he read on, he became convinced that he was "the unknown beloved" to whom the letter was addressed! It seemed that his mistress loved him; she commanded him to always wear cross-gartered yellow stockings and always

smile in her presence. "Thy smiles become thee well," he read.

"Jove I thank thee," cried the duped steward, kissing the letter. "I will smile; I will do everything that thou wilt have me."

Poor Malvolio believed that Olivia might marry him. He rushed to his room to change his stockings and then he sought Olivia out. Smiling as broadly as he was able,

he started to strut up and down in front of her, showing off his yellow cross-gartered stockings. Olivia, who knew nothing of the letter, thought he had gone mad.

"Wilt thou go to bed, Malvolio?" she asked kindly.

"To bed, ay sweetheart; and I'll come to thee," said Malvolio, winking and kissing his hand.

"God comfort thee," cried Olivia, growing more concerned. "Why dost thou smile so and kiss thy hand so oft?"

Malvolio quoted whole sentences from the letter, but still Olivia looked bewildered. Finally, she gave orders that he be locked up in a dark room till he had recovered his senses. Poor Malvolio was carried off kicking and shouting at such injustice.

In which Olivia declares her love.

Later that day, Viola arrived at Olivia's home, still acting as Orsino's page. She bowed deeply to Olivia and said that she had come to tell her of Orsino's love.

Again Olivia refused to listen to Orsino's suit, rejecting him entirely. The only person Olivia wanted to wed was Orsino's page, but every time she tried to woo the page, the page talked of Orsino.

"I love thee so," Olivia eventually burst out, abandoning all pretence of pride.

Viola was horrified and didn't know how to answer Olivia.

"I am not what I am," Viola insisted at last. She tried to rush away, and swore to herself that she would never again be her master's messenger.

"Yet come again!" cried Olivia, as Viola finally managed to flee from the house.

Sir Andrew overheard this exchange. He, like Duke Orsino, had been rejected

by Olivia on countless occasions. He realized that Olivia was in love with the duke's page and he went off angrily to complain to Sir Toby.

"Marry, I saw your niece do more favours to the count's serving-man than ever she bestowed upon me," he grumbled.

Sir Toby was most concerned; if Sir Andrew gave up trying to court his niece,

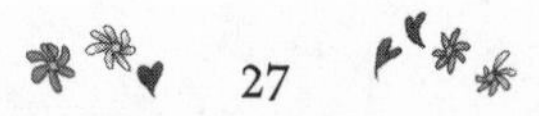

he might lose his supply of wine! He encouraged Sir Andrew to challenge this new rival to a duel. "Hurt him in eleven places: my niece shall take note of it," he assured his friend.

In which Sebastian makes the confusion worse.

Meanwhile Viola's twin, Sebastian, hadn't drowned after all. He had been washed up on the shore some way down the coast and had been rescued by a sea captain called Antonio, an old enemy of Orsino's. Like Viola, he thought his twin was dead, and he mourned her deeply. To distract him, Antonio persuaded him to go and explore the town. Antonio was nervous, because

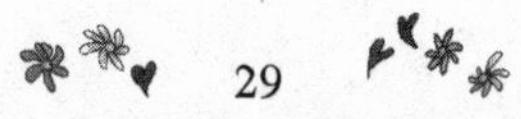

if he was discovered by the duke's men he would be arrested, so he went to look for discreet lodgings while Sebastian toured the local sights. Antonio, knowing that

Sebastian had no money, lent him his purse and arranged to meet him later at a certain inn. Antonio had forgotten that he would need his purse to secure their lodgings, so he soon found himself chasing after Sebastian, who seemed to have vanished down a maze of narrow streets.

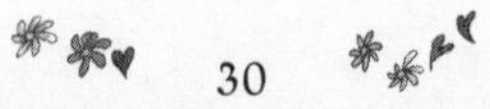

Eventually he found Sebastian, and was astonished to see that he was fighting! Little did Antonio realize this was Sebastian's twin, Viola, duelling with Sir Andrew. Antonio rushed to "Sebastian's" defence.

"If this young gentleman have done offence, I take the fault on me," he declared gallantly.

"You, sir! Why, what are you?" cried Sir Toby.

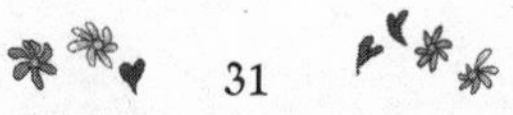

As fate would have it, some soldiers were standing close by. Before the argument could be settled, they recognized Antonio as the duke's enemy and arrested him.

"Antonio, I arrest thee at the suit of Count Orsino," said the officer.

"You do mistake me, sir," lied Antonio.

"No, sir, no jot: I know your favour well," returned the officer.

Antonio asked "Sebastian" to return his purse so that he could buy his freedom. Viola, who had never seen Antonio before, was astonished at his request and refused.

"What money, sir?" she asked, in all innocence.

Antonio could not believe that the youth he had dragged from the surf and befriended should repay his kindness in this way.

"Thou hast, Sebastian, done good feature shame," he ranted at Viola in a fury, as the soldiers dragged him away.

Viola stood thunderstruck. This man had used Sebastian's name! He must know her brother, and her brother must still be alive! In a whirl of excitement, Viola fled back up the hill to Duke Orsino's house.

Sir Andrew, who had stood by and watched all this, felt cheated of his duel. So he and Toby chased Viola – but they ended up catching Sebastian! Sebastian had carried on sightseeing, unaware of all the drama. He was innocently wandering past Olivia's home, admiring its fine design, when Sir Andrew marched up to him and slapped him in the face!

"Now, sir, have I met you again? There's for you," Sir Andrew cried.

"Why, there's for thee, and there, and there!" yelled Sebastian, beating Sir Andrew as hard as he could. "Are all the people mad?"

Seeing Sir Andrew sink to his knees, Sir Toby grabbed hold of Sebastian and tried to calm him.

"Come on sir, hold," he pleaded.

All the men were in a fury now, and within minutes, all three drew their swords.

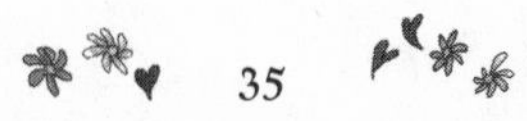

They were making such a racket that Olivia rushed from her house to see what the commotion was about.

"Hold, Toby! On thy life I charge thee, hold!" she cried in horror, thinking that Sir Toby was about to run his sword through her beloved. She chased her uncle and Sir Andrew into the house and then turned to

the man she believed to be Orsino's page. She begged him not to go, but to stay and hear about her love for him. Sebastian couldn't make out if he was in a dream or if everyone had indeed gone mad. He guessed that Olivia loved him through some mistake, but he had no desire to resist her advances!

"If it be thus to dream, still let me sleep," he declared happily.

"Would thou'dst be ruled by me!" smiled Olivia.

"Madam, I will," replied Sebastian, too bemused to argue.

"O say so, and so be!" exclaimed Olivia.

Olivia couldn't believe that her page might return her love at last. So, rather than let

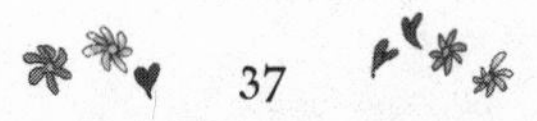

the moment pass and risk losing him again, Olivia rushed Sebastian to the town church to be married.

In which the mysteries are resolved.

After the wedding, the confused but happy Sebastian left his new bride while he went in search of Antonio to return his purse.

At the same time, Duke Orsino, who knew nothing of the wedding, set out with Viola to beg the countess Olivia to marry him! On their way to Olivia's house, they met Antonio being marched to jail by two officers. Viola pointed him out to the duke as the gentleman who had rescued her from a duel. But Antonio pointed at Viola and cried, "That most ingrateful boy there by your side denied me mine own purse!" Viola denied all knowledge of the purse and the duke dismissed Antonio's claim. Then Olivia appeared and all else

flew from Duke Orsino's thoughts.

"Here comes the countess," he gasped. "Now heaven walks on earth!"

Olivia ignored the duke, for she only had eyes for his page, who she kept referring to as her "husband"! This made both duke and page gasp.

"Her husband, sirrah!" shouted the duke in a fury. "O, thou dissembling cub!"

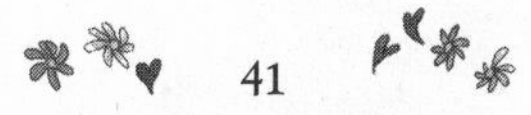

The duke was furious to think that his trusted page had stolen his countess. He might have set about Viola if Sir Toby and Sir Andrew hadn't hobbled up, both moaning loudly and shaking their fists at Viola.

"He has broke my head across, and has given Sir Toby a bloody coxcomb too," complained Sir Andrew.

"Why do you speak to me? I never hurt you," swore Viola.

Then, as if by magic, another boy who looked just like the page was seen wandering up the street towards them! Everyone fell silent and everyone stared.

"One face, one voice, one habit, and two persons," uttered the duke in confusion.

"How have you made division of yourself?"

wondered Antonio. "An apple cleft in two is not more twin than these two creatures."

Then, as Viola embraced Sebastian, the confusion began to clear – the page was not a boy at all, but this young man's sister!

"Most wonderful!" exclaimed Olivia, throwing her arms around Sebastian. For she realized with relief that Sebastian was her true husband and not the dissembling Viola.

Duke Orsino was stunned and looked at his page in utter astonishment. He

might have been furious, but instead he remembered Viola's tenderness towards him and realized that she must have loved him from the first. So he gave up his wasted love for Olivia and offered his heart to Viola, who felt close to fainting with happiness.

"Give me thy hand; and let me see thee in thy woman's weeds," smiled her duke.

In high good humour, the duke pardoned Antonio for his past misdeeds and Sebastian gave him his purse back. Olivia wanted everyone to share in her happiness, so she called for her steward to be released.

"Madam," Malvolio cried.

"You have done me wrong. Notorious wrong."

"Have I, Malvolio? No," insisted Olivia. But no amount of explaining would convince Malvolio that his mistress was not part of the plot against him.

"Alas, poor fool, how have they baffled thee!" sighed Olivia.

"I'll be revenged on the whole pack of you!" Malvolio cried, and he marched off, his cross-gartered yellow stockings flashing through the evening gloom.

Not even Malvolio's furious departure could cast a shadow over the rest of the company. As Olivia's jester, Feste, began to sing a song of celebration, everyone except Malvolio linked arms in love and friendship. The terrible shipwreck on Illyria's shores had turned out to have a silver lining.

William Shakespeare was a popular playwright, poet and actor who lived in Elizabethan England. He married in Stratford-upon-Avon aged eighteen and had three children, although one died in childhood. Shakespeare then moved to London, where he wrote 39 plays and over 150 sonnets, many of which are still very popular today. In fact, his plays are performed more often than those of any other playwright, and he died 450 years ago! His gravestone includes a curse against interfering with his burial place, possibly to deter people from opening it in search of unpublished manuscripts. It reads, "Blessed be the man that spares these stones, and cursed be he that moves my bones." Spooky!

Marcia Williams' mother was a novelist and her father a playwright, so it's not surprising that Marcia ended up an author herself. Although she never trained formally as an artist, she found that motherhood, and the time she spent later as a nursery school teacher, inspired her to start writing and illustrating children's books.

Marcia's books bring to life some of the world's all-time favourite stories and some colourful historical characters. Her hilarious retellings and clever observations will have children laughing out loud and coming back for more!

More retellings from Marcia Williams

ISBN 978-1-4063-5692-2

ISBN 978-1-4063-5693-9

ISBN 978-1-4063-5694-6

Charles Dickens'
David Copperfield
Retold and Illustrated by
Marcia Williams

ISBN 978-1-4063-5695-3

Available from all good booksellers

www.walker.co.uk